To Liam, Myra, Nora & Ou[...]

Home is anywhere you

can READ!

DL Speer

First published in the United States of America

by Allifish Press. For information or orders,

visit www.allifishpress.com

First edition
ISBN 978-1-5323-7713-6

Editor's note
This story was inspired by a wild turkey. In the
early 2000s, it could often be seen in the
neighborhood adjacent to the Fort Worth Zoo
in Fort Worth, Texas. The Zoo often received
calls to warn them "their turkey" had escaped.

To Caroline and Casey,
my daily inspirations for
pretty much everything.

Theodore
the turkey who found a zoo

by Allison F. Speer

There once was a turkey named Theodore who lived in a lovely neighborhood.
His home was nestled among beautiful, two-story houses, big magnolia trees and straight sidewalks up and down the streets.

When Theodore walked along those sidewalks, all the people who lived in the cozy, charming homes would say, "Hello, Theodore!" or ask, "How's it going, Theodore?" He would gobble back, hoping for an invitation inside or maybe to be asked to join a game of soccer. He wanted so badly to live in one of those houses. To call it his home. The people were friendly, but only with a wave that said "Hello." Not a wave that said, "Come inside!"

One day as Theodore was strolling and strutting through the homey, restful neighborhood, he heard a loud *"RRROOOAAARRR!"*

Intrigued, he followed the sound through the gray pathways. He crossed a busy street. He kept following the *ROAR!* because he was so curious. Maybe he was a little frightened, but mostly just curious.

Finally, Theodore's path led him to a large gate that read, "City Zoo."

(Side note: Turkeys who live in human neighborhoods read the newspapers that lay on sidewalks in the early mornings, so they become quite fluent.)

He paraded up to the ticket window to pay admission, but the ticket seller looked down at him and asked, "How long have you been on break? Get back in your exhibit and start gobbling!"

Theodore cocked his head to one side and blinked. He

blinked again. Then he thought, *"Hey! Free admission!"*

So in through the turnstiles he went.

Theodore came upon an exhibit full of zebras. He hopped up on the cement wall, and then stepped on to the soft grass. *Hmm,* he thought. *Maybe this is where I'm supposed to be. Perhaps, this is my neighborhood.*

"Love your stripes," he said to a nearby zebra who was chewing the soft grass. But the zebra slowly looked up, rolled his eyes and huffed. "Oh please, feather boy. Go on and be a bird. This spot is for stripes only."

So Theodore skittered back from the grass, stepped on to the cement wall and leapt back on to the wide, bumpy path, looking for the bird exhibit.

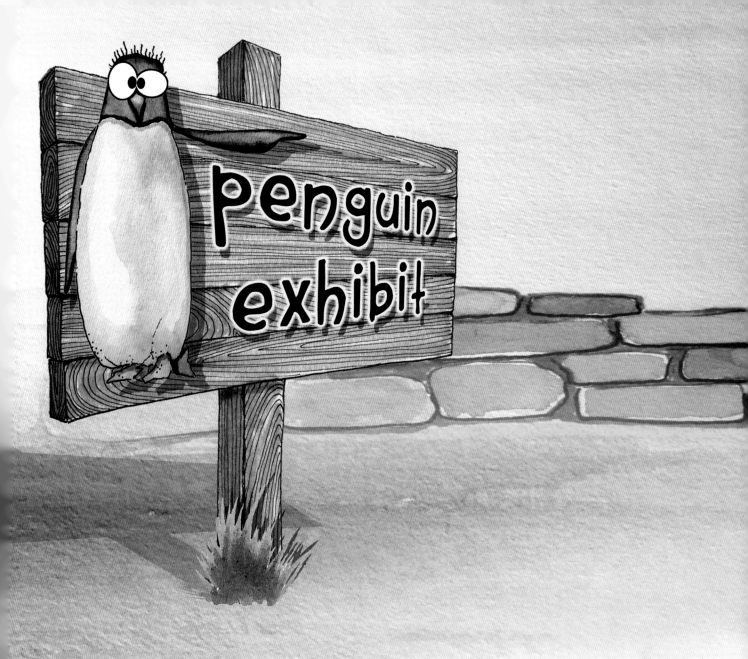

"*PENGUINS,*" Theodore read aloud as he walked up one, two, three steps and entered the chilly, dim room. He saw black and white birds waddling, diving, eating fish and swimming with friends. *Birds!* He said to himself.

Maybe this is my home!

Theodore stepped up to the thick glass window and tapped his beak. *Tap, tap, tappity tap.* "Hey!" he announced. "How do I get in there? Birds of a feather stick together, right?"

And then he watched as
the penguins
toppled over
like bowling pins.
Laughing, giggling, howling, bowling pins.
"You gotta be kidding!" one chubby
penguin laughed.
"We ain't birds! We can't fly!"
Then he pointed his wing toward Theodore and called
to his friends. "Hey guys, he thinks penguins can fly!"

The rest of the penguins laughed even more. And laughed. And laughed. Theodore slowly stepped away from the thick glass and made his way back down the steps out to the wide, bumpy path. But he wasn't really strutting so much anymore. His eyes were focused on his feet below him as he watched them move one in front of the other.

I guess that's not where I belong, either, he thought.

He heard the sound that originally led him to the zoo.

"It's a sign!" He told himself. *"Maybe this is where I belong!"*

So he straightened his feathers, wiggled his waddle, picked the flecks of dirt from between his toes and gobbled his loudest *GGGGGOOBBLE GOBBLE GOBBLE!* to the large animal lyin' in the grass. Standing on the bench that overlooked a vast plot of greenness and a sun-covered plateau, Theodore prepared to introduce himself, certain this was where he belonged.

'Hello, I'm Theodore, and I heard your call from a mile away.
'm certain that you and I are one of a kind. We both have
beautiful clothes, majestic calls and it looks like you enjoy
sitting in the sun like me. Mind if I stay?"

The lazy lion raised his large head and yawned so that Theodore could see his many white, sharp, pointy teeth. Then he licked his lips with his fat, pink tongue and spoke. "Theodore, you will be wise to notice that you do not have a mane like mine."

The lion then shook his head back and forth so that the fur surrounding his face fluffed and flurried like the petals surrounding a sunflower.

"And unless you have an appetite for meat," the lion said as he started to stir and stand, "then you'll want to find your way out. It's dinner time, and I'm quite hungry. *ROAARRRR!*"

Although the lion didn't laugh at him, and he wasn't rude, Theodore took the hint and thought it best to exit quickly before he became an early Thanksgiving meal.

Where is my home? He wondered. *Where do I belong?* *No one looks like me, sounds like me, or even wants to be my friend.*

Theodore waddled back on to the bumpy road. Feeling dejected and rejected, he began to wander again. He must have been watching his feet, one in front of the other, because he suddenly bumped into a tree.

Only it wasn't a tree. It was the long, lanky leg of the zookeeper man.

"Hey there, turkey," the tall man said. "You look like that gobbler who lives in the neighborhood up the street. People call us about you all the time. They think you belong to us, but I always tell them the turkey's turf is not here in our territory."

Theodore and the tall man began to walk and talk. They walked and talked. They talked and walked.

That day, Theodore and the man became friends. Every time Theodore would leave the zoo to go back to the streets with the cozy homes, the man stared at his beautiful plumage (that's a fancy word for display of feathers). The man stared and thought. He stared and thought, and he thought and stared.

The next few weeks, Theodore began making weekly visits to see the zookeeper man. He knew they weren't the same kind, but that didn't seem to matter. They liked each other. They were friends.

One day when Theodore visited the zoo - always free of charge - walking the bumpy path with his tall friend, they stopped in front of a small yard carved into a tiny little corner of the park, next to a restaurant. It was far from the snobby zebras and the pesky penguins and the lazy lions.

"I have a surprise for you, Theodore," the tall man announced.

Theodore looked ahead and saw a fancy wooden sign. It read, *"Theodore the Turkey, Resident of the City Zoo."*

Theodore was so delighted that his plumage plumed and his gobbler gobbled and his eyes lit up like the stars over the vast, Texas night sky. He had found a neighborhood. A place he could call home.

One evening after all the guests had left and the zookeepers had clocked out, a few of the penguins waddled over to his yard. They asked him to teach them to read.

What he wanted to say, more than anything in the world, was to remind them that if penguins couldn't fly, they certainly couldn't read!

Theodore the Turkey
Resident of
the City Zoo

He started giggling. He giggled and gobbled. And then his memory took him to the time when his eyes followed his feet down the path. A time where he had no home, and he felt alone. He never wanted anyone to feel like he did that day.

He looked at the penguins. He strutted and strolled.
He strutted and strolled. He strolled and strutted.
Then he pointed to his sign and said, "This is the
letter T. T stands for Theodore. And that's me.
Maybe not everyone can fly, but just about anyone
-- even a penguin -- can read."

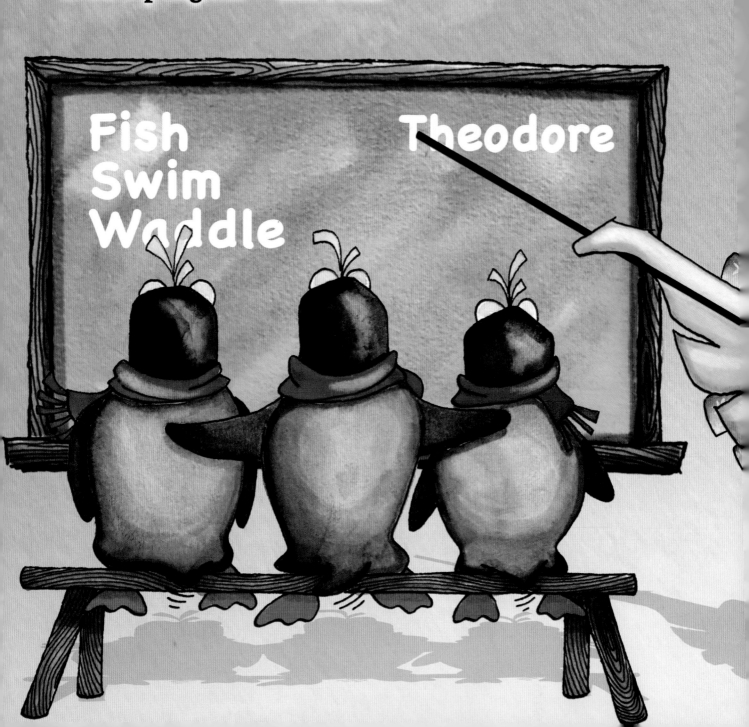

The End